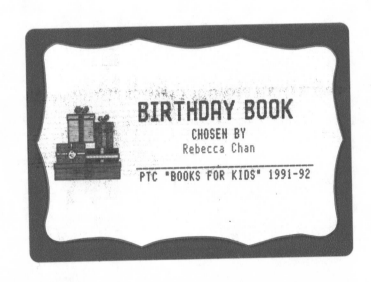

BIRTHDAY BOOK
CHOSEN BY
Rebecca Chan

PTC "BOOKS FOR KIDS" 1991-92

MAMA CAT'S YEAR

NORMA SIMON Illustrated by DORA LEDER

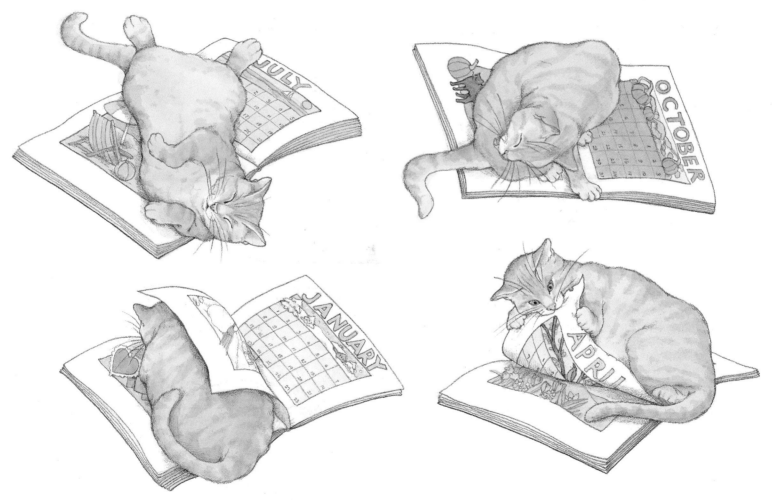

ALBERT WHITMAN & COMPANY • Morton Grove, Illinois

Mama Cat's year has four seasons—
winter,
spring,
summer,
and fall.
Mama Cat loves them all.

She doesn't know the names
of the months
the way *I* do,
but she knows when the seasons change.
How does she know?

Her eyes see it.
Her ears hear it.
Her nose smells it.
Her fur feels it.
Her tongue tastes it.

Day by day, little by little,
when winter comes,
Mama Cat knows.
How does she know?
Her coat grows thicker,
until she looks like a big orange ball.
She sniffs the damp air, just before it snows.
She hears the north winds blow,
and her ears stand up.
She watches icicles drip and drop.
She licks the ice, and her tongue sticks to it.

When it snows,
Mama Cat sniffs the snow on her fur.
She licks the white flakes melting on her nose.

She pounces into the big snowdrifts
and sinks over her head.
She shakes the snow off her icy paws.
She rides on my sled!

Sometimes Mama Cat says, "Let me out, please."
But she doesn't like it when the wind
blows hard and the cold rain soaks her fur.
She wants to come back in *right away*.

She finds a puffy quilt and
catnaps where it's very warm.
Mama Cat knows
winter is a good time for snoozing.

Day by day, little by little,
when spring comes,
Mama Cat knows.
How does she know?
She sniffs and chews the new green grass.
She rolls over and over,
wriggling in the softness.

Mama Cat sheds her heavy winter coat.
Big fur clumps fall out—
on the floor, on the bed, everywhere!
Mama Cat's thin spring coat is cool and sleek.

It's time to check Mama Cat for ticks and fleas.
She squirms and tries to run away.
She hates to be checked,
but she hates fleas and ticks, too,
so we just *have* to do it!

Mama Cat sniffs the fresh earth while Dad digs our garden.

She scratches the tree bark while Mom hangs wet clothes.

She chases the ball when I'm up at bat.

She's busy and frisky and funny in springtime.

Day by day, little by little,
when summer comes,
Mama Cat knows.
How does she know?
She listens to the buzzing sound of bees.
She watches butterflies fly by.
She sniffs and licks the heavy morning dew,
and she eats the newly cut grass
while Mom mows the lawn.

Last summer, Mama Cat became a mama.
I was there when her kittens were born—
a boy kitten with gray fur,
a boy kitten with black fur,
a girl kitten with brown fur,
and a girl kitten with orange fur, just like Mama Cat.
She fed her baby cats and taught them
to hunt and keep clean and play cat games.

Soon the kittens grew bigger,
and they were ready to move to new homes.
Mama Cat missed her babies. I did, too!
She searched for them everywhere in our house.
Then she got used to being our only cat again.

This summer Mama Cat walks along
the garden fence like a careful tightrope walker
while we pick green beans,
green cucumbers, and green zucchini.

Mama Cat watches us swim,
but she runs away when we splash!
On long, hot days, she pussyfoots
into cool, dark shadows.

Day by day, little by little,
when fall comes,
Mama Cat knows.
How does she know?
She hears Dad chop wood.
She sniffs the fresh logs.
She watches the big yellow bus
pick me up for school,
and she waits for me to come home.
She feels the air grow cool,
and her fur grows thick again.

When squirrels are storing winter acorns,
Mama Cat scares them right up the trees.
When we rake leaves into giant piles,
Mama Cat jumps in, just like me.

She watches us gather apples and pumpkins.
She sniffs the steaming pots of fruit.
She sees us cut our jack-o-lanterns.

When children come for Trick-or-Treat,
Mama Cat arches her back.
She's afraid of the funny Halloween costumes,
so she looks and runs away.
I think she meets with other cats
who feel exactly the same!

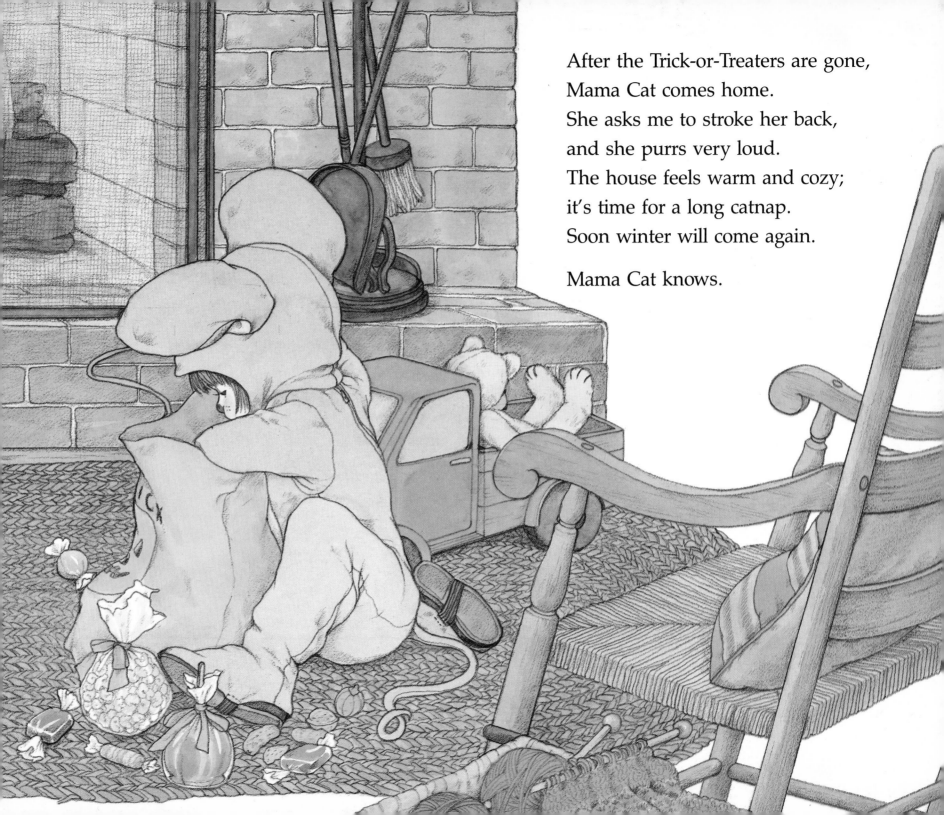

After the Trick-or-Treaters are gone,
Mama Cat comes home.
She asks me to stroke her back,
and she purrs very loud.
The house feels warm and cozy;
it's time for a long catnap.
Soon winter will come again.

Mama Cat knows.

The text typeface is Palatino
and the display typeface is ITC Novarese.

The illustrations are watercolor and pencil.

Designer: Karen Johnson Campbell.

Library of Congress Cataloging-in-Publication Data
Simon, Norma.
Mama Cat's year/Norma Simon; pictures by Dora Leder.
p. cm.
Summary: Describes, season by season, the life of a
cat and her human family over one year.
ISBN 0-8075-4958-4
[1. Seasons—Fiction. 2. Cats—Fiction.] I. Leder,
Dora, ill. II.Title.
PZ7.S6053Mam 1991   90-26825
                                          CIP
                                          AC